I'm a Little Superhero

by Danielle R. Gordon
Illustrated by Chad Vivas

I'm a little
Superhero

By Danielle R Gordon

Illustrated by Chad Vivas

I'm a little Superhero
Copyright © 2016 Danielle Ranae Gordon

ISBN-13: 978-0692775363
ISBN-10: 0692775366
Afro Princess Publishing

In memory of Ronald 'Ronnie' Gordon

Dedicated to all the Afro Princes

My name is little Ronnie, and I'm a superhero. My super power is helping people.

Dad calls me his little superhero because
I always save the day.

Like the one time I saved my little
brother from the vacuum cleaner.

Or the day I rescued mommy from a giant spider.

And I always save the day by helping
Grandpa find his teeth when he
misplaces them.

As a superhero, I have to be ready to help people. That's why I eat lots of fruits and vegetables so I can stay healthy.

I also have to exercise so that
I can stay strong.

And I exercise my brain to keep it alert.

I like being a superhero. Helping people makes me feel good.

Anyone can be a superhero.

You can be one too.

THE END